JE
Ben Kemoun, Hubert. JAN   2010
The boomerang wakes up

The Adventures of Sam X

THE BOOMERANG WAKES UP

by Hubert Ben Kemoun

illustrated by Thomas Ehretsmann

translated by Genevieve Chamberland

STONE ARCH BOOKS
www.stonearchbooks.com

First published in the United States in 2009
by Stone Arch Books,
151 Good Counsel Drive, P.O. Box 669
Mankato, Minnesota 56002
www.stonearchbooks.com

Library of Congress Cataloging-in-Publication Data
Ben Kemoun, Hubert, 1958–
 [Reveil du boomerang. English]
 The Boomerang Wakes Up / by Hubert Ben Kemoun; illustrated by
Thomas Ehretsmann.
 p. cm. — (Pathway Books Editions. The Adventures of Sam X)
 Originally published: Le reveil du boomerang. France: Nathan, 2003.
 ISBN 978-1-4342-1222-1 (library binding)
 [1. Boomerangs—Fiction. 2. Supernatural—Fiction.] I. Ehretsmann,
Thomas, ill. II. Title.
PZ7.B4248Bo 2009
[Fic]—dc22   2008031578

Summary: Sam's adventurous uncle left tons of treasure behind. So when
Sam finds a boomerang given to Uncle Julius by an Australian sorcerer,
he can't wait to try it out. But when the boomerang is used, it wakes up!
It has a taste for kangaroo meat, it can't be put back to sleep . . . and now
it's chasing Sam!

Creative Director: Heather Kindseth
Graphic Designer: Emily Harris

1 2 3 4 5 6 14 13 12 11 10 09

Printed in the United States of America

TABLE OF CONTENTS

Chapter 1

THE TREASURE CHEST

I knew that Lionel and I weren't supposed to be in the guest room when Uncle Julius wasn't there.

Uncle Julius was a world traveler. Sometimes, when he wasn't traveling, he came to visit me and my mother.

Whenever he came to visit, he stayed in the guest room. When he was gone, he left some of his personal belongings there.

The guest room closet was stuffed with Uncle Julius's things. There were clothes, photographs, and souvenirs from his trips around the world.

Uncle Julius was always traveling. My mom had agreed to keep his treasures in our apartment until he stopped traveling and settled down. Uncle Julius was an adventurer. I didn't think he would ever stop traveling.

I was digging in a big metal chest in the guest room. Like I said, I knew I wasn't supposed to be in there, but I just needed to find one thing.

"I think I found it!" I said.

"What are you talking about?" asked Lionel. "What did you find?"

"I'm talking about this!" I said. I stood up, holding a small, flat leather bag.

Lionel frowned. "What's that?" he asked.

"Uncle Julius brought it back from Australia," I said. "He got it from a sorcerer there."

"What is it?" Lionel asked.

"It's very special and extremely dangerous," I told him. "That's what the sorcerer told Uncle Julius when he gave it to him."

"Okay, but what is it, Sam?" Lionel asked. I could tell that he was getting annoyed with me.

"It's a weapon," I told him. "It's for hunting kangaroos."

I reached into the leather bag and pulled out a boomerang. It was incredible! It was carved from a dark, hard wood. The edges of the boomerang were sharp. It was very thin.

Lionel frowned. He didn't seem very impressed. He just looked at the boomerang and asked, "What are you going to do with that boring old piece of wood?"

"I'm going to try it out, of course!" I said.

"What else would I do with it?"

Lionel bent down and picked up a piece of paper. It had fallen out of the boomerang's bag. "What's this?" he asked.

Lionel unfolded the piece of paper. There was writing on it.

He read it to himself. Then he looked at me. I could see that Lionel was worried.

"You need to put that thing away right now, Sam," he said. "Really. It's dangerous. Even your uncle Julius says so. This note is from him. See for yourself!"

I snatched the piece of paper away from Lionel.

I read the note. It was from Uncle Julius. It said:

Light as a hummingbird,

fast as a bullet,

quick as an arrow,

it is as hungry as an eagle.

It hunts for the kangaroo.

Never awake this sleeping boomerang! Never!

Julius

I laughed when I finished reading the note. My uncle was such a joker. He was just trying to scare me so I'd stop looking through his stuff when he was gone.

"He's just kidding around," I told Lionel. "He's trying to scare us so we'll stay out of his stuff, that's all."

Lionel didn't look so sure. "What if it's true?" he asked.

I laughed again. "How many kangaroos have you seen around here?" I asked.

"None," Lionel admitted. "But . . ."

"Stop worrying," I told him. "Come with me!"

Chapter 2

BY THE RIVER

Lionel and I went down to the river. I wanted to try out the boomerang.

Lionel still didn't think it was a good idea. The letter had freaked him out.

"The boomerang is not going to work," he told me. "Those things never work!"

"Quit bugging me," I said. "Just let me try it out!"

Lionel frowned. "Don't expect me to run over to the other side of the field and get it," he grumbled.

I shook my head. "You don't have to get it," I said. "That's what's magical about a boomerang. It comes back to you!"

Lionel sighed. "It's never going to work," he said.

I ignored him. The boomerang in my hand weighed less than a feather.

Lionel hopped up and down. He was getting nervous.

"Hurry up, Sam!" he said. "We shouldn't have gone into your uncle's room. We shouldn't have gone through his things. And this note makes me really worried!"

"Here it goes!" I said.

I swung my arm in a half-circle. The boomerang spun as it flew away, high in the sky.

"It's going to fall," Lionel said angrily. "You threw it way too hard. This is stupid, Sam."

I shook my head. "It'll turn around," I said. "Just you wait and see."

We watched, squinting up into the sky. Suddenly, just as I hoped, the boomerang started to turn. Before we knew it, it was headed back toward us.

"I can't believe it!" Lionel whispered.

I stared at the boomerang as it flew back toward us. I reached out, ready to catch it.

"This is crazy!" Lionel said. "I can't believe this is happening!"

I shook my head. "It's normal," I told him. "It's a boomerang! That's what they're supposed to do!"

The boomerang slowed down as it came closer. It was headed right for me. I was sure that I was going to be able to catch it.

Suddenly, just before it reached my hands, the boomerang turned.

It flew to the left. It crash-landed on top of our jackets. We'd left them in a pile on the ground.

"That's too bad, but still, it was really cool!" Lionel said. "It was just your first try. I bet that the next one will work better."

"I don't get it," I said. "Why did it turn all of a sudden?"

Lionel shrugged. "It was probably just the wind," he said.

I walked over to pick up the boomerang. That's when I saw what had happened to my jacket.

The boomerang had slashed a big hole in my new jacket. The hole had ripped right through one of the jacket's sleeves.

I sighed. "My mom is going to be so mad," I said, looking at the sleeve. "This is a new jacket!"

I put it on, trying to get a better look at the damage. It didn't look good. My mom was not going to be happy.

Lionel came over and reached out his hand. "Come on, give me that thing," he said. "I bet I can throw it better than you!"

I handed the boomerang to Lionel. He moved away and stood so that he was facing the wind.

When he tossed it, the boomerang flew up above the ground. It turned around perfectly, high in the sky.

It flew straight toward Lionel. I was sure he was going to catch it.

Then, at the last second, it changed. Just like it had when I threw it, suddenly, the boomerang turned!

This time, it was different. It didn't land on the ground. I couldn't explain what was happening.

The boomerang started to speed up. It was flying faster and faster. I couldn't believe how fast it was flying.

It was coming straight toward me!

Chapter 3

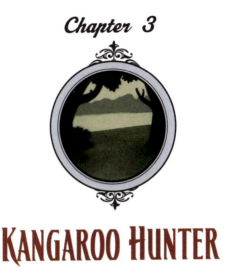

KANGAROO HUNTER

"Run, Sam! Run!" Lionel yelled.

I did what he said. I ran, screaming, away from the boomerang.

I could hear it behind me, whistling as it flew closer and closer, following me. I was running as fast as I could.

The boomerang wasn't losing speed. It seemed like it was going faster.

I was terrified!

No matter what I did, even if I suddenly tried to change direction, the boomerang followed me.

I could hear the boomerang spinning behind me. It seemed like someone was controlling it with a remote control, but no one was around.

All I knew was that no matter what I did, the boomerang followed me. It wanted to catch me!

Lionel ran behind me. He yelled, "Sam! Get under the trees! Hurry!"

I turned toward the river. There were trees lining the banks. As I turned, I could hear the boomerang following me.

I hoped that the boomerang would hit a tree branch. Then it would stop chasing me.

When I ran under the trees, the boomerang didn't run into any branches. Instead, it sank down.

It flew close to the ground. Then the branches were way too high. They couldn't stop it.

I kept running along the shore of the river as quickly as I could. I was starting to get really tired.

I felt trapped. I didn't know where to go or where to hide.

I slid between trees. I jumped over big rocks.

The boomerang just kept following me. I could not escape.

Sweat dripped down my face. I wanted to cry, but I was running too fast.

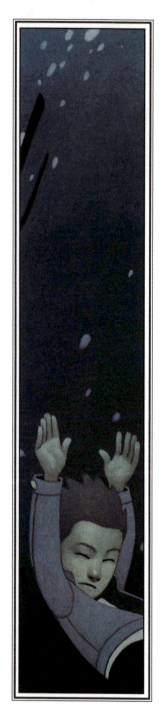

I could hardly breathe. I felt like my heart was going to explode as I ran alongside the river.

There was only one thing left to try. Without stopping to think, I jumped into the shallow, icy river.

Behind me, I heard a splash. It was the boomerang, following me into the water.

I screamed because the water was so cold. I started choking.

Lionel jumped in after me. He pulled me out and laid me on the shore.

I was soaking wet. And Lionel was just as wet as I was.

I looked back. The boomerang was floating quietly. It was stuck in the tall weeds on the shore of the river.

Who would have believed that a simple, small piece of wood had almost killed me? Who would have thought that the little, V-shaped toy had wanted to destroy me?

I sat down on a rock, trying to calm down and catch my breath. I took my jacket off so that I could squeeze the water out of it.

Lionel was on the beach of the river. He stuck a long, dead branch into the water. He was trying to fish out the boomerang.

I shivered. "Please, don't wake it up!" I said nervously.

Lionel looked at me. "I think it's okay unless we throw it," he said. "When we carried it here earlier, nothing happened. We'll just put it back in its bag and take it to your house."

He scooped the boomerang out of the water. Then he walked toward me, holding onto the strange weapon with the tips of his fingers, as if he were holding onto a poisonous spider.

"Come on, Sam," Lionel said. "Let's go back to your place and put on some dry clothes. I'll borrow some stuff from you."

Suddenly, he stopped in his tracks. His eyes were wide, and he kept looking back and forth between me and my jacket, lying on a rock to dry.

"Oh no," Lionel whispered. "I think I figured it out, Sam. The kangaroo is you!"

He looked shocked by what he'd discovered. I didn't know what he was talking about.

I kept looking at my jacket, and then back at Lionel. I didn't get it.

"What are you talking about?" I asked.

"The buttons!" Lionel croaked. "Your buttons! Look at the buttons!"

I shook my head. "Are you going crazy?" I asked.

Lionel just stood there, looking nervous. "The buttons," he repeated quietly.

I got up to take a closer look at my jacket.

The buttons on my jacket were made of steel. Each one was engraved with the words "Sydney Clothing" in a circle around the edge. And inside the circle was a little, tiny kangaroo.

I had never looked at the buttons on my jacket before. But somehow, the magic and crazy boomerang had seen those tiny kangaroos.

Chapter 4

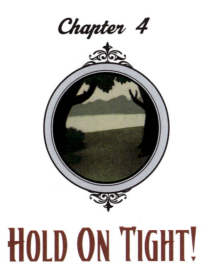

HOLD ON TIGHT!

We started walking back toward my apartment building. To get home, we decided to take the dirt path next to the river, instead of climbing up the hill to the main road.

I slipped on my wet, torn jacket, but I was still freezing.

"You're holding onto it tight, right?" I asked Lionel.

"Don't worry," Lionel said. "I'm holding it so tight it's making my hands hurt."

Our shoes looked like aquariums, and our socks looked like rags. I could tell that Lionel wasn't feeling any better than I was. He kept sniffing and sneezing.

"I don't know why you didn't believe your uncle's note," he said. "I don't know why you thought he was making up the story about the boomerang."

"Don't mention that word!" I said.
"I don't want to think about that thing.
Are you sure you're holding onto it really
tight?"

"I'm sure," Lionel said.

"I just want to get it back to my
apartment, put it back in its little bag,
and lock it up in Uncle Lionel's room,"
I said. "The sooner we can get rid of it,
the better!"

"Then let's cross the road right here,"
Lionel said. "We'll get back faster that
way."

The road we were near was the
highway. It was really dangerous to cross.
We couldn't cross the road there. Trucks
and cars were speeding down the road.
We'd never make it.

On the way to the river, we had crossed the highway by going into a little tunnel. But we probably wouldn't reach the tunnel for another fifteen minutes.

If we crossed here, we'd save time. I was desperate to get home, change my clothes, and hide the horrible boomerang for once and for all.

"Okay," I said. "We can cross here."

The highway looked like a large, powerful river. Lionel and I stood next to the railing, wondering how to cross the road.

Cars and trucks kept flying by. There wasn't a break in the traffic at all.

A truck passed us, only inches from our noses. "It's too dangerous!" I yelled to Lionel. "We'll never make it!"

Lionel looked down the highway. "Get ready," he said. "We have to run after the green car goes by. Then we have to stop in the middle, but we'll be safe there," he added. He got ready to run.

"No way!" I said. "I already almost died once today. That was enough for me!"

"But if we go all the way to the tunnel, it'll take at least twenty minutes," Lionel said.

I shook my head. "I don't care," I said. "Twenty minutes isn't worth losing our lives!"

Just then, a huge truck honked and passed by us. It was going so fast that the wind almost knocked us over. I jumped and fell backward.

As I fell, I grabbed Lionel's arm. He fell down with me.

As we tumbled down the slope, Lionel let go of the boomerang. "Sam!" he yelled. "Watch out!"

The boomerang had taken off above us. The wind pushed it up. The boomerang sped off, spinning in the air.

The nightmare was starting all over!

"Your buttons, Sam. Tear off your buttons!" yelled Lionel. "Come on, hurry up!"

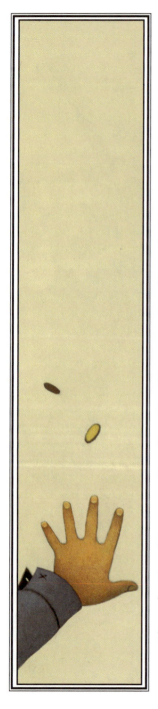

I was already running. As quickly as I could, I started pulling my jacket buttons off.

I glanced behind me and screamed. The boomerang was already starting to turn around and head toward me.

My coat had six buttons. I pulled each of them off. Then I tossed each one in a different direction.

Every time I threw a button, the boomerang slowed down for a second. Then it would charge toward the steel button.

Even if I threw a button far away, the boomerang would chase it and shatter it. Then it would quickly start chasing me again.

I threw the last button away from me, and the boomerang dove for it. It shattered the button just before it knocked into a big tree.

I thought that would be it, but no! The boomerang was still hungry!

I was panicking. I looked down at my jacket, searching for more kangaroos.

Then I spotted them. There were buttons on the sleeves of my jacket, too! I ripped them away.

I threw the two wrist buttons as hard as I could. The boomerang dove for them and destroyed them.

Finally, I thought it was over. I thought the boomerang would fall down and stop its crazy chase. But instead of landing on the field next to the river, the boomerang flew up, higher into the sky. Soon, all I could see was a tiny dark dot in the sky.

Lionel was out of breath when he caught up to me. "We woke it up," he said quietly. "Now it's hunting."

"For how long?" I asked. I looked over at Lionel, but he was staring up into the sky.

"It's coming back down!" he yelled. "It's getting faster!"

Lionel was right. The boomerang was coming down really fast, and it was headed straight for me and Lionel.

He looked over at me. "Quick, did you forget a button?" he asked.

"No!" I shouted. "I took them all off, I swear!"

Lionel seemed hypnotized by the boomerang, diving toward us at the speed of light. I knew what I had to do.

Run!

Chapter 5

THE KANGAROO'S GRAVE

I pulled Lionel up, and we ran toward the river. I was ready to jump into the freezing water, but the water was deeper here and the current was really strong.

I didn't know what to do. I stopped at the edge of the water and turned around. I looked up into the sky, trying to see where the boomerang was.

It was only a few feet away from me, and it was headed straight for my heart!

I jumped into the mud next to the river just in time. The boomerang tore my jacket as it passed by.

It was going really fast, so it couldn't stop. But before it reached the other side of the river, it turned around.

I knew it was coming back for me. It wasn't done yet. But I didn't care. I stayed in the mud.

I was too tired to run anymore. I wanted to give up.

Lionel wasn't giving up! He pulled my jacket off by the shoulders.

Suddenly, through the hole the boomerang had made in my jacket, I saw it.

There was a label inside my coat. It had a kangaroo on it.

That kangaroo looked just like the kangaroos on the buttons, but it was bigger. That was what the boomerang wanted. That's what it was chasing!

Lionel tore the label out. A large piece of the lining of my jacket got ripped out at the same time.

The boomerang that was charging at me suddenly changed direction. It quickly turned around.

"Lionel, watch out!" I yelled. "It's behind you!"

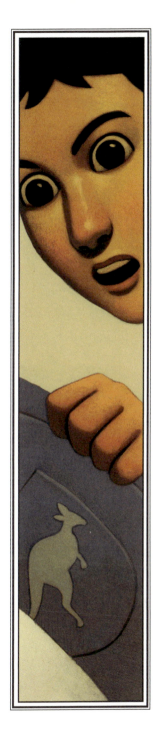

My friend dove into the mud next to me just as the boomerang was about to cut his hand off.

Once again, the boomerang crossed the river and turned around on the other side. It was ready to charge at us again.

We tried to roll over to get farther away from the boomerang, but we were stuck in the mud. We had no strength left.

That was it. The boomerang was going to win the game.

But instead of diving at us again, the boomerang rose up above the river and started to fly in circles in the sky. It was searching for something.

That's when I saw that Lionel's arm was buried in the mud, up to his elbow.

He must have still had the piece of fabric in his hand, and it was too deep for the boomerang to find it. The hunting boomerang knew that the kangaroo was down there, but it couldn't figure out how to get to it.

"Bury it deeper!" I told Lionel.

Lionel shook his head. "The boomerang might still come down here," he said. "It won't work."

"That's exactly what I want!" I told him. "Come on, help me!"

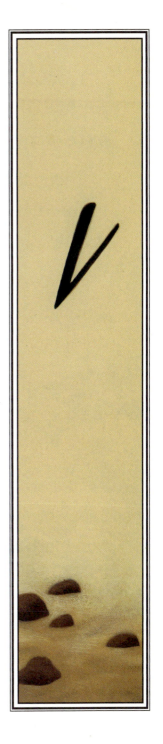

I grabbed a long, dead branch. I poked it into the mud and pushed the piece of my jacket deeper.

Then Lionel and I rolled a big rock to the mud. We used it to cover up the hole the stick had made.

Finally the kangaroo's grave was finished. We got up and ran away from the spot.

"Over here!" Lionel whispered. We hid behind a tree so that we could watch what would happen.

High above the river, the angry boomerang kept on circling. It was watching, and getting angrier and angrier.

Then it started to go faster than it ever had before. It dove down to the mud.

The landing was incredible! The boomerang exploded in pieces against rocks that had been hidden in the mud.

Lionel and I went back to my house without saying a word. We were glad to be safe, but we were also soaked, dirty, and tired. And my jacket was in a million pieces.

When we got to my apartment, my mom yelled at us. Then she locked Lionel and me in the bathroom. She said we couldn't come out until we cleaned ourselves up.

"Don't worry," I told Lionel as we washed our faces. "My mom's screams aren't as bad as the boomerang. She's not as mad at us as the boomerang was with the kangaroos."

"What about your uncle?" Lionel asked. "Won't he be mad when he finds out that you took his boomerang?"

I laughed. "I think he'll be glad I'm alive, even if his boomerang isn't," I said. Then I stopped laughing. "At least I hope he will," I said.

Lionel didn't look so sure. And I wasn't either.

THE END

About the Author

Hubert Ben Kemoun was born in 1958 in Algeria, on the northern coast of Africa. He has written plays for radio, screenplays for television, musicals for the stage, and children's books. He now lives in Nantes, France, with his wife and their two sons, Nicolas and Nathan. He likes writing detective stories, and also creates crossword puzzles for newspapers. When he writes stories, he writes them first with a pen and then copies the words onto a computer. His favorite color is black, the color of ink.

About the Illustrator

Thomas Ehretsmann was born in 1974 on the eastern border of France in the town of Mulhouse (pronounced mee-yoo-looz). He created his own comic strips at the age of 6, inspired by the newspapers his father read. Ehretsmann studied decorative arts in the ancient cathedral town of Strassbourg, and worked with a world-famous publisher of graphic novels, Delcourt Editions. Ehretsmann now works primarily as an illustrator of books for adults and children.

GLOSSARY

belongings (bi-LONG-ingz)—things that someone owns

boomerang (BOO-muh-rang)—a curved stick that can be thrown through the air so that it returns to its owner

current (KUR-uhnt)—the movement of water in a river

damage (DAM-ij)—harm done

desperate (DESS-pur-it)—willing to do anything to change the situation

hypnotized (HIP-nuh-tized)—in a trance

kangaroo (kang-guh-ROO)—an animal from Australia with short front legs and long, powerful back legs that are good for leaping

magical (MAJ-ik-uhl)—having special powers

poisonous (POI-zuhn-uhss)—able to kill or harm someone

shallow (SHAL-oh)—not deep

sorcerer (SOR-sur-er)—someone who performs magic

souvenirs (soo-vuh-NEERZ)—things that you keep to remind you of a person, place, or event

MORE ABOUT BOOMERANGS

Nobody knows the exact orgins of the boomerang, but it has been around for thousands of years.

Many people believe that boomerangs are native to Australia. However, they were used in ancient Egypt, Europe, and the United States as well.

The original boomerang was basically a throwing stick. It was much heavier and straighter than modern boomerangs. It was used as a weapon during hunting to kill or scare the animals.

Today the boomerang is used for sport. It comes in many different colors, designs, sizes, and materials.

Like there are for most sports, there are many different boomerang tournaments and contests.

Every other year, a boomerang world cup is held. It is an international competition.

During boomerang competitions, there are many different events. Some events test for distance, while others test for endurance and accuracy. One event is a timed test to see how fast the player can throw and catch his or her boomerang five times.

The throwing technique is important during any boomerang event. It takes practice and concentration. It is very different from throwing a flying disc.

DISCUSSION QUESTIONS

1. Was it okay for Sam and Lionel to be in Uncle Julius's room? Why or why not?

2. Lionel and Sam finally stopped the boomerang by burying the fabric kangaroo in the sand. What else could they have done to escape from the boomerang?

3. Why do you think Sam wanted to find the boomerang in Uncle Julius's room? Talk about your answers.

Writing Prompts

1. There are a lot of cool things in Uncle Julius's room. Make up an object that could be found there and write a story about it. Where did Uncle Julius get it? What can it do? What would happen if it was found? Write about it!

2. Lionel is Sam's best friend. Write about your best friend. What do you like about your friend? What do you like to do together?

3. Do you think Uncle Julius will be mad when he finds out that the boomerang has been destroyed? Write a story that tells what happens when Sam tells his uncle the bad news.

More Sam X Adventures!

The Adventures of Sam X

Whimsical, colorful, and intense, these chapter books follow the surreal life of Sam X. Join Sam X and his best friend, Lionel, as they embark on strange adventures — controlling the weather, losing a shadow, and watching a snake tattoo come to life!

Visit www.stonearchbooks.com

INTERNET SITES

Do you want to know more about subjects related to this book? Or are you interested in learning about other topics? Then check out FactHound, a fun, easy way to find Internet sites.

Our investigative staff has already sniffed out great sites for you!

Here's how to use FactHound:

1. Visit *www.facthound.com*

2. Select your grade level.

3. To learn more about subjects related to this book, type in the book's ISBN number: **9781434212221**.

4. Click the **Fetch It** button.

FactHound will fetch the best Internet sites for you!